Fancy NANCY

STORYBOOK FAVORITES

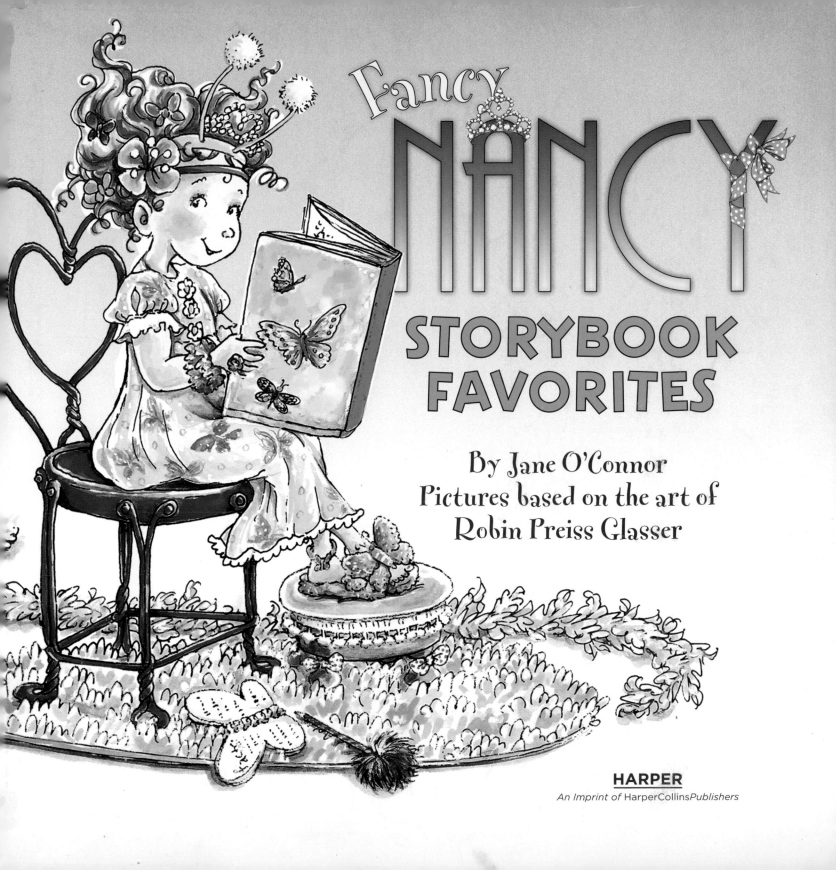

Fancy NANCY

STORYBOOK FAVORITES

By Jane O'Connor
Pictures based on the art of
Robin Preiss Glasser

HARPER
An Imprint of HarperCollinsPublishers

Table of Contents

97 Fancy Nancy and the Delectable Cupcakes

Fancy Nancy: The Show Must Go On

129

161

Fancy Nancy: The Dazzling Book Report

Fancy NANCY

and the Late, Late, LATE Night

I adore visiting my neighbor Mrs. DeVine.
Here we are having tea on her veranda.
(That's a fancy word for porch.)

When she was a child, Mrs. DeVine lived in Hollywood. She used to see lots of movie stars—only Mrs. DeVine calls them celebrities.
Isn't that fancy?

She has a special scrapbook of photographs.
Some are autographed.
That means celebrities signed them.

"Your scrapbook is extremely fascinating," I say.
(Fascinating is even more interesting than interesting.)

Ooh la la! Mrs. DeVine says I can borrow her scrapbook if I bring it back tomorrow. "Merci, merci, merci!" I say.

At home I pretend that I am a Hollywood celebrity.
I dress up in my most glamorous attire—that's fancy for clothes.

13

I give my autograph to all my fans.

I pose for photographs.

"I am late for a glamorous Hollywood party," I tell my fans.
"Au revoir!"
(You say it like this: aw ruh-VWA. That's French for "good-bye.")

On my door I put up a sign that says
Do Not Disturb,
because celebrities need their privacy.
I want to look through Mrs. DeVine's scrapbook,
but I hear my dad calling us all to dinner.

After dinner I learn all my spelling words.
I am practically an expert at spelling.
Before I know it, Mom says, "Nancy, time for bed."
Oh no! I haven't had a second to look at the scrapbook.

I beg my mom to let me stay up later. But my mom says no.
"It's a school night. Tomorrow is Friday.
Tomorrow you can stay up later."

19

I put on my nightie and get in bed.

My parents kiss me good night.
"Sleep tight," they say.

But guess what! I am not going to sleep.
Under the covers, I have concealed—
that's fancy for hidden—
a flashlight and the scrapbook.

I stay up very late.

It is almost ten o'clock when I put away the scrapbook and turn off my flashlight.

I bet even celebrities don't stay up this late!

The next morning, when my dad wakes me up,
I am exhausted. Exhausted is even worse than tired.

At recess, I am too exhausted to jump rope with Bree and my friends.

I miss three of the words on the spelling list.
My brain is exhausted, too.

After school, I return Mrs. DeVine's scrapbook.
She asks if I would like to stay for dinner
and watch a movie called *National Velvet*.

"It is on TV tonight. It is about a girl and a horse.
I loved it when I was your age," she says.
It sounds fascinating, but I can hardly keep my eyes open.

I go home and start weeping—which is fancy for crying.
When my dad asks what's wrong, I confess.
"I was naughty. I stayed up late last night and
I had a terrible and exhausting day."

My dad doesn't scold me. He says, "Now you understand why you need a good night's sleep."

That night I go to bed even earlier than my sister!

On Saturday I wake up feeling glorious again.
(Glorious is fancy for wonderful.)

And guess what—Mrs. DeVine taped the movie for me!
I can see it tonight.

Dad was right—even fancy girls need their beauty rest.

"Class, don't forget!"

Ms. Glass says.

"Tomorrow is . . ."

"Pajama Day!" we shout in unison.

(That's a fancy word

for all together.)

I plan to wear my new nightgown.

I must say, it is very elegant!

(Elegant is a fancy word

for fancy.)

Then the phone rings.

It is Bree.

She says, "I am going to wear
my pajamas with pink hearts
and polka dots.

Do you want to wear yours?

We can be twins!"

"Ooh!" I say.

"Being twins would be fun."

Then I look at my elegant nightgown.

What a dilemma!

(That's a fancy word for problem.)

Finally I make up my mind.

I tell Bree I am going to wear

my brand-new nightgown.

Bree understands.

She is my best friend.

She knows how much

I love being fancy.

The next morning at school,

we can't stop laughing.

Everyone's in pajamas,

even the principal.

He is carrying a teddy bear.

Ms. Glass has on a long nightshirt

and fuzzy slippers.

I am the only one

in a fancy nightgown.

That makes me unique!

(You say it like this: you-NEEK.)

"Nancy, look!" says Bree.
"Clara has on the same
pajamas as me."

Bree and Clara giggle.

"We're twins!" says Clara.

"And we didn't even plan it."

At story hour, Ms. Glass

has us spread out our blankets.

She reads a bedtime story.

Clara and Bree lie
next to each other.
"We're twins,"
Clara keeps saying.

At recess

Clara takes Bree's hand.

They run to the monkey bars.

"Come on, Nancy," Bree calls.

But it is hard to climb in
a long nightgown.
And I can't hang upside down.
Everyone would see
my underpants!

At lunch

I sit with Bree and Clara.

They both have grape rolls

in their lunch boxes.

"Isn't that funny, Nancy?"
asks Clara.

"We even have the same dessert."

51

I do not reply.

(That's a fancy word for answer.)

Pajama Day is not turning out

to be much fun.

I wanted to be fancy and unique.

Instead I feel excluded.

(That's fancy for left out.)

The afternoon is no better.

Clara and Bree are partners

in folk dancing.

Robert steps on my hem.
Some of the lace trim
on my nightgown rips.

At last the bell rings.

I am glad Pajama Day is over.

"Do you want to come
play at my house?"
I ask Bree.

But Bree can't come.

She's going to Clara's house!

I know it's immature.

(That's fancy for babyish.)

But I almost start to cry.

Then, as we are leaving,

Bree and Clara rush over.

"Nancy, can you come play too?"

Clara asks.

"Yes!" I say.

"I just have to go home first to change."

Now we are triplets!

Fancy Nancy's Fancy Words

These are the fancy words in this book:

Dilemma—a problem

Elegant—fancy

Excluded—left out

Immature—babyish

Reply—answer

Unique—one of a kind (you say it like this: you-NEEK)

Unison—all together

Stars are so fascinating.

(That's a fancy word

for interesting.)

I love how they sparkle in the sky.

Tonight is our class trip.

Yes! It's a class trip at night!

We are going to the planetarium.

That is a museum

about stars and planets.

Ms. Glass tells us,

"The show starts at eight.

We will all meet there."

I smile at my friend Robert.

My parents are taking Robert and me.

Then Ms. Glass asks,

"What star is closest to Earth?"

That's easy.

It's the sun.

"What do you call stars
that make a picture?"
asks Ms. Glass.
Robert and Bree have both forgotten.
"I know, I know," I say.
"A constellation."

Ms. Glass nods.

On the wall are pictures.

There's the hunter and the crab

and the Big Dipper.

It looks like a big spoon.

We will see all of them at the show.

I can hardly wait.

THE BIG DIPPER

At home, Robert and I
put glow-in-the-dark stickers
on our T-shirts.
Mine has the Big Dipper.
Robert has the hunter on his.

We spin my mobile

and watch the planets orbit the sun.

(Orbit is a fancy word.

It means to travel in a circle.)

Then we pretend to orbit

until we get dizzy.

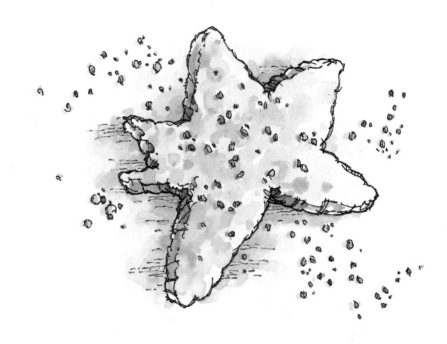

Later, we bake star cookies.

Sprinkles make them sparkle.

"The sun is a star,"

I tell my sister.

"It is the closest star,

so we see it in the day."

After dinner,

we wait for the baby-sitter.

She is very late.

Dad says not to worry.

We have plenty of time.

At last we get in the car.

Drip, drip, drip.

It is raining.

The rain comes down
harder and harder.
Dad drives slower and slower.
It is getting later and later.

A policeman comes over.

"The road is closed,"

he tells my parents.

"There is too much water."

Oh no!

There are cars in front of us.

There are cars behind us.

We are stuck!

"The show is starting soon!"

Robert says.

"We will not make it."

Drip, drip, drip goes the rain.

Drip, drip, drip go my tears.

Robert and I are so sad.

We do not even want any cookies.

At last the cars move

and the rain stops.

But it is too late.

The night sky show is over.

By the time we get home,

the sky is full of stars.

They are brilliant!

(That's a fancy word

for shiny and bright.)

I get a brilliant idea.

(Brilliant also means very smart.)

We can have

our own night sky show.

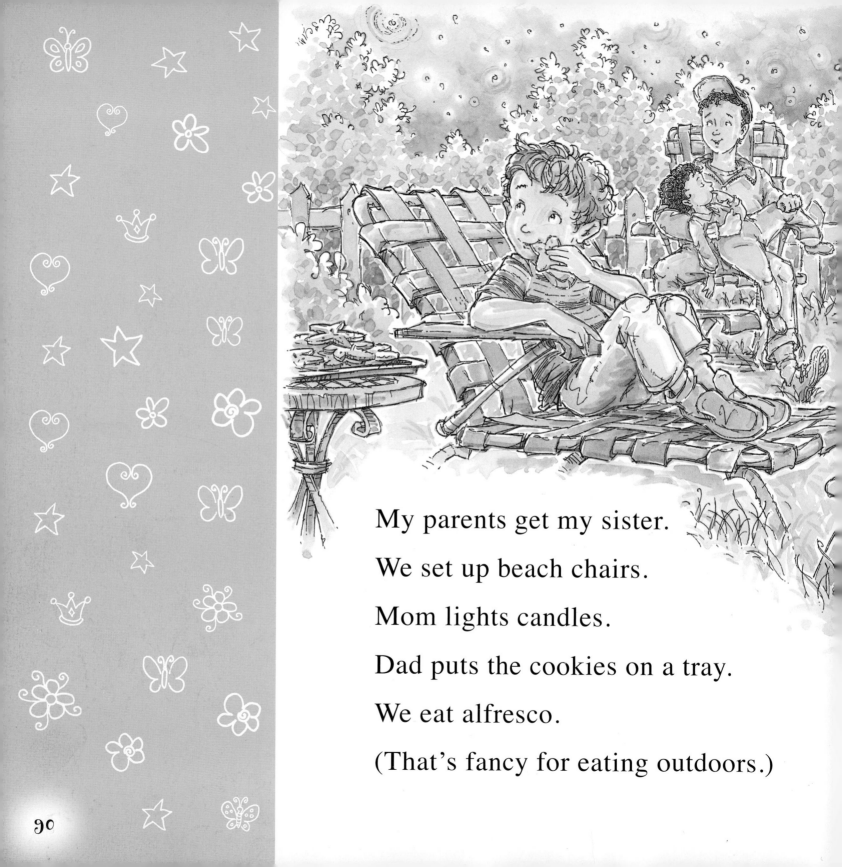

My parents get my sister.

We set up beach chairs.

Mom lights candles.

Dad puts the cookies on a tray.

We eat alfresco.

(That's fancy for eating outdoors.)

We watch the stars.

We see the North Star.

We see the Big Dipper.

All at once,

something zooms across the sky.

"A shooting star," Dad says.

"Make a wish!"

I tell Dad it is not a star.

It is a meteor.

But I make a wish anyway.

The next day Ms. Glass says,

"Everyone missed the show

because of the storm.

So we will go next week."

Everybody is very happy.

And guess what? My wish came true!

Fancy Nancy's Fancy Words

These are the fancy words in this book:

Alfresco—outside; eating outside is called eating alfresco

Brilliant—bright and shiny, or very, very smart

Constellation—a group of stars that make a picture

Fascinating—very interesting

Meteor—a piece of a comet that leaves a blazing streak as it travels across the sky (you say it like this: me-tee-or)

Orbit—to circle around something

Planetarium—a museum about stars and planets

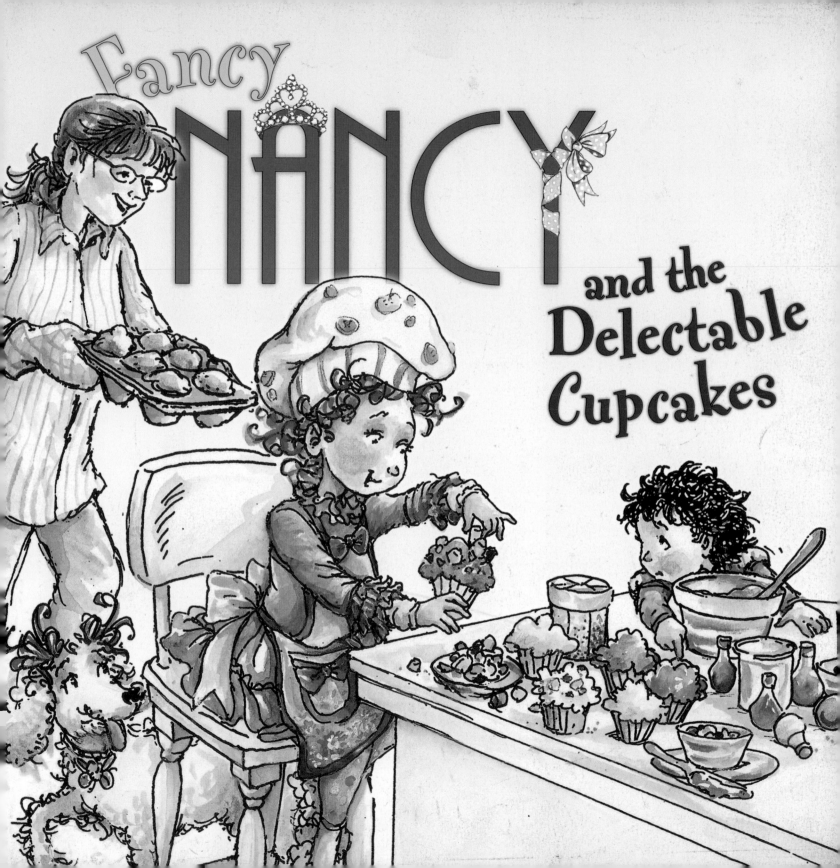

Fancy NANCY

and the Delectable Cupcakes

I adore school.

(Adore means to really,

really like something.)

But today I can't wait to go home.

I am going to bake cupcakes—

fancy cupcakes.

"Nancy, did you hear
what I just said?" Ms. Glass asks.
I shake my head.
"I will repeat it," Ms. Glass says.
(Repeat is fancy for saying
something over again.)
"There is no recess tomorrow
because of the bake sale."
The bake sale is to raise money
for library books.

Before I leave,

I go over to Ms. Glass.

"I am sorry.

I wasn't being a good listener."

Ms. Glass smiles.

"I know you are trying to improve."

(Improve is fancy for

getting better at something.)

I hug Ms. Glass.

I adore her. Really I do.

On the way home

Bree says she is making brownies

for the bake sale.

Robert is making a red velvet cake.

It is not really made with velvet.

(That is a very fancy kind of cloth.)

But the inside is all red.

"I will definitely buy a piece,"

I tell him.

At the market, my mom buys
eggs and milk,
flour and sugar,
and butter.

"Don't forget sprinkles and candy,"
I tell her.

It's lucky I am here or we would
end up with plain cupcakes!

I want to start baking right away.

I listen carefully to my mother.

Ms. Glass would be very proud.

I put all the right stuff in the batter.

I pour the batter into the cupcake pan.

My sister is not such a good listener.
My mom tells her three times
to keep her fingers out of the batter.

The cupcakes come out of the oven.

Ooh la la! What a lovely aroma!

(Aroma is fancy for smell.)

When they cool off we put on

frosting and sprinkles and candy.

I want to show Mrs. DeVine my cupcakes.

My mom says, "Come back soon.

And be sure to leave the cupcakes

where Frenchy can't get them."

I am already out the door.

Mrs. DeVine buys a cupcake.

She says it is delectable.

(That is fancy for yummy.)

I come home and call Bree.

We make a deal.

I will buy two of her brownies.

She will buy two of my cupcakes.

I hope I sell all of them.

A minute later I hang up.

Then I see Frenchy's face.

Frosting is all over her mouth!

Oh no!

The cupcakes are a mess.

"Nancy, didn't you listen?"

my mom asks.

"I said to leave them in a safe place."

"It is all my fault.

I wasn't listening,"

I tell my mom.

Just then my dad comes home.

I tell him what happened.

"Now I don't have cupcakes

for the bake sale."

"Cupcakes?" my dad says.

"You baked cupcakes already?"

Then he holds out a big bag.

In it is all the stuff for cupcakes.

"I told you I would buy everything,"

both my parents say at the same time.

Then they start laughing.

I laugh too.

Nobody in my family is a good listener!

After dinner

we bake cupcakes all over again.

I am exhausted.

(That's fancy for very tired.)

My dad says,

"Nancy, please get ready for bed."

Guess what?

For once, he doesn't have to

repeat himself!

The bake sale is a big success.

My cupcakes are all gone.

"Oh!" I say to my mom.

"I didn't even get to taste one."

"Look!" my mom says.

She saved one for me.

I taste it.

Mmm. Totally delectable.

Fancy Nancy's Fancy Words

These are the fancy words in this book:

Adore—to really, really like something

Aroma—a smell

Delectable—yummy

Exhausted—very tired

Improve—to get better at something

Repeat—to say something over again

Velvet—a very fancy kind of cloth

"Quiet, please," says Ms. Glass.

"I have an announcement."

(That means she has something

important to tell us.)

"The talent show is in a week."

Yay! Bree and I bump fists.

We have our act planned out already.

We will wear fancy circus costumes.

We will sing a song.

It is about daring girls on a trapeze.

Then Ms. Glass says,

"I am assigning partners."

Oh no!

That means we don't get to choose!

I am not assigned to Bree.

I am assigned to Lionel.

He is very shy.

I hardly know him.

Ms. Glass wants us

to brainstorm with our partner.

That means to talk over ideas.

So I ask Lionel,

"Do you like to sing?"

He says no.

He does not like to dance

or tell jokes.

He can wiggle his ears.

 He can crack his fingers.

He can balance a spoon on his nose.

"Very cool," I say.

"But I can't do those things.

We need to perform together."

(Perform is a fancy word for act.)

That night I say,

"Bree and Yoko are partners.

They will do a fan dance

and wear kimonos."

(I explain that a kimono

is a fancy Japanese robe.)

"Lionel and I
can't think of anything to do."
I sigh a deep sigh.
"And now I won't get to wear
my circus costume."

Mom says, "Ask Lionel over.

Get to know each other.

It will help you plan an act."

On Saturday I ask Lionel over.

But his mom can't drop him off.

So Dad drives me to Lionel's house.

Ooh la la! It is very fancy.

It is almost a mansion.

Lionel's room is huge.

(Huge is much bigger than big.)

There are lots of toy lions.

"Oh! I get it!" I say.

"You like lions

because your name is Lionel."

I pick up a little glass lion.

"This is adorable," I say.

I tell him I like fancy words.

And adorable is fancy for cute.

Lionel shows me a lion mask.

"Wow," I say. "It's great!"

He puts on the mask.

"Grrr," Lionel says, and chases me.

We race all over his house.

"Help! Help!" I yell.

149

Later we have snacks.

"You're a great lion," I tell Lionel.

Then I get an extremely great idea!

"Let's do a circus act.

You can be the lion.

I can be the lion tamer.

I already have a costume."

Lionel likes the idea. Yay!

The next week we get together

many times to rehearse.

(That's a fancy word for practice.)

Still, we are nervous
on the day of the show.
We hear Ms. Glass announce,
"Here is Lady Lulubell
and the man-eating lion!"

The curtain opens.

Lionel jumps through the hoop.

Lionel walks on a pretend tightrope.

Then he roars and chases me.

"Don't eat me!" I cry.

"Eat this instead!"

I hand Lionel a huge lollipop.

He starts licking it and purring.

Then I curtsy and he bows.

Our act is over.

There is a lot of applause!

(That's a fancy word for clapping.)

I hear my dad shout, "Bravo!"

We all go out for ice cream.

I give Lionel a clay lion I made.

And guess what?

He teaches me

to balance a spoon on my nose!

Fancy Nancy's Fancy Words

These are the fancy words in this book:

Adorable—cute

Announcement—something important to tell

Applause—clapping

Assign—to choose something for someone else

Brainstorm—to talk over lots of ideas

Bravo—way to go!

Kimono—fancy Japanese robe

Mansion—a very fancy house

Perform—to act (or dance or sing)

Rehearse—to practice

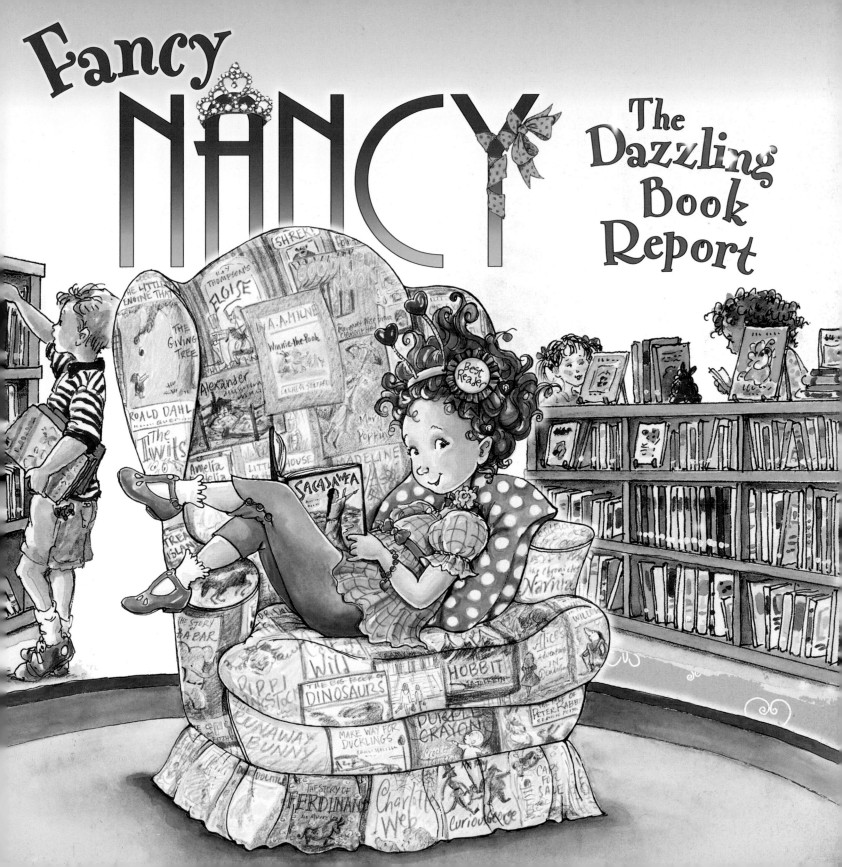

Monday is my favorite day.

Why?

Monday is Library Day.

Before we leave, we select a book.

(Select is a fancy word for pick.)

It is like getting a present

for a week!

Bree selects a book on dinosaurs.

Robert selects a book
of funny poems.

Teddy selects a scary story.

I select a book
about an Indian girl.
She has a fancy name,
Sacajawea.
You say it like this:
SACK-uh-jah-WAY-ah.

Later Ms. Glass has

thrilling news.

(Thrilling is even more exciting

than exciting.)

We get to do a book report!

"Your first book report.

How grown up!"

my mom says at dinner.

"Yes, I know," I say.

"My book is a biography.

It is about a real person."

After dinner I read my book.

Dad helps with the hard words.

I learn all about Sacajawea.

Sacajawea was a princess.

She lived two hundred years ago
out West.

She helped two explorers
reach the Pacific Ocean.

Mom takes me to the art store.

I need stuff for

the cover of my book report.

I want it to be great!

(I am the second-best artist

in our class.

This isn't bragging.

You can ask anybody.)

I get a bag of little beads,

some yarn,

and markers.

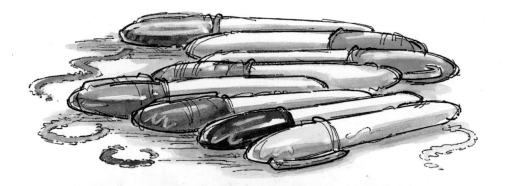

I start working on the cover.

I work on it every night.

I make Sacajawea look very brave,

because she was.

She found food for the explorers.

She kept them safe from enemies.

"Just remember to
leave time for the words,"
Mom keeps saying.
"I will. I will," I tell her.

"Ms. Glass wants you
to write about the book,"
Dad says over and over.
"That's what a report is."
"I know that!" I tell him.
Writing the words will be easy.

Ta-da! The cover is finished.

Sacajawea has yarn braids.

Beads and fringe are glued
on her clothes.

I must admit it is dazzling.

(That is fancy for eye-popping.)

Now I will write my report.

I get out lined paper

and a pen with a plume.

(That's a fancy word for feather.)

The trouble is, I am tired.

I know all about Sacajawea.

But the right words won't come.

What am I going to do?

I have to hand in my report tomorrow!

"I am desperate!" I tell Mom.

(That means I'm in trouble.)

Mom lets me stay up longer.
Still my report ends up
only two sentences long.

The next day,
everyone sees my cover
and says, "Wow!"

But hearing other reports
makes me nervous.
All of them are longer
than mine.
All of them are more interesting.

I read my report.

"Sacajawea was a heroine.

She helped people in trouble."

Everybody waits to hear more.

But there is no more.

I am crestfallen.

(That is fancy for sad and ashamed.)

"I spent too much time

on the cover,"

I tell Ms. Glass.

Ms. Glass understands.

"Why don't you tell the class about your book?"

So I do.

I tell them all about

the brave things Sacajawea did.

Sacajawea was a heroine.

Ms. Glass is a heroine too.

At least, she is to me!

Fancy Nancy's Fancy Words

These are the fancy words in this book:

Biography—a story about a real person

Crestfallen—sad and ashamed

Dazzling—eye-popping, a knockout

Desperate—feeling trapped

Heroine—a girl or a woman who is brave and helps people

Plume—feather

Select—to pick

Thrilling—even more exciting than exciting